HORACE MORRIS

BY LINDA HELLER

MACMILLAN PUBLISHING CO., INC. / NEW YORK

COLLIER MACMILLAN PUBLISHERS / LONDON

When the second hand touched twelve and it was exactly five o'clock, Horace Morris rang Emmaline Potterton's doorbell. She had invited him for dinner at five, and his behavior was always perfect.

But there was no light in the hallway and no sound of footsteps came to the door. No one was home.

Horace looked at his watch. Where was Emmaline? Where was her father? Where was her mother? Where was his dinner? Had something horrible happened to the Pottertons, or had they forgotten all about him? Horace didn't like to be kept waiting and was hurt and upset.

"I certainly hope they come soon," Horace told the Potterton's dog.

Half an hour later, Emmaline Potterton skated up the street.

"Hi, Horace," said Emmaline. "Sorry to be late, but I lost one of my wheels racing home. I finally found it and was putting it back on when a small, rough tongue licked my ear."

"A small, rough tongue?" asked Horace.

"That's right," answered Emmaline. "A cat was in my knapsack."

"Oh," said Horace.

"This isn't just any old cat," said Emmaline. "She's the most beautiful cat in the city, the state, the country, the world, maybe even the universe! I knew her owner would be worried, so I rushed right to the police station."

"That was very considerate," said Horace, "and exactly the right thing to do."

"When I got there," continued Emmaline, "I saw a man crying and muttering, 'Only one minute from fame, and now this. Only one inch from stardom, and now this. Oh, Jasmine. We came so close, so close!'

"Well," said Emmaline, "I went right over to cheer him up, and immediately he started smiling and clapping his hands. 'Jasmine, Jasmine,' he said. 'Oh, no,' I said. 'I'm Miss Emmaline Esther Potterton.' But he wasn't talking to me at all."

"Who was he talking to?" asked Horace, somewhat suspiciously.

"To the cat in my knapsack, of course," answered Emmaline. "To Jasmine, the world's greatest tap-dancing cat. She had gotten lost on the way to their big break...."

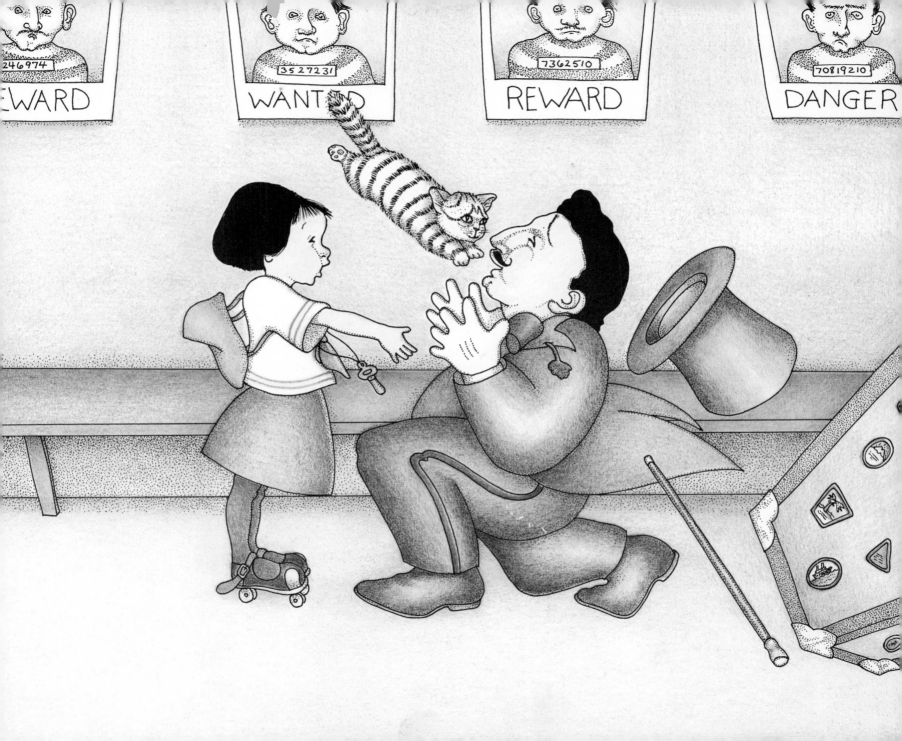

"Excuse me," said Horace, who was always very polite. "But a tap-dancing cat? Cats are known for their soft paws and their quiet steps."

"That's why they have to wear special tiny tap shoes," said Emmaline, putting her fingers together to show the size of Jasmine's shoes.

Horace didn't believe a word of this and wondered why Emmaline had made up such a ridiculous story. Just then, Mrs. Potterton dashed up the street.

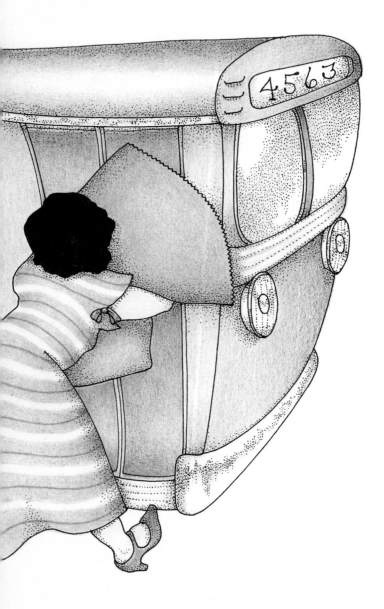

"Sorry to be late," she gasped, "but you must hear what happened. I wanted to make one of my delicious dinners, so after work I ran to the market and squeezed every melon, examined each string bean, picked the plumpest frankfurters and the biggest chocolate cake. Then I rushed and caught the bus.

"As I sat there thinking how nice it would be to see you again, Horace, something whizzed by and tickled my nose."

"Tickled your nose?" asked Horace.

"The bus was so crowded," continued Mrs. Potterton, "that all I could see were my groceries. But then a woman called out, 'Claude! Come back, my precious.' And a man yelled, 'Watch those cages.'"

"Cages?" said Horace. "What cages?"

Mrs. Potterton went on. "Then Claude and I met, because he landed on my grocery sack and began to eat the chocolate cake and squawk, 'Needs more icing. Needs more cherries.'"

"Pardon me," said Horace rather loudly, "but I still don't understand about the tickling and Claude and the cages and...."

"What?" said Mrs. Potterton looking confused. "Didn't I mention that before? Claude is a cockatoo. Actually, there were two cockatoos. The other one kept chattering, 'Step to the rear. Step to the rear.' But nobody did.

"By this time there was so much confusion that the driver was forced to pull over. Then the birds flew out the window, their owner ran out after them, and we continued on our way."

"Oh, my," said Horace, thinking Mrs. Potterton's story was even sillier than Emmaline's.

But, because he was very polite, Horace said, "Mrs. Potterton, please let me help you with the groceries."

"Why, thank you, Horace," she said, and they all went inside.

Just as they reached the kitchen, Mr. Potterton came home.

"Sorry to be late," he said, "but I had quite a time getting here.

"The traffic was terrible, and when I reached Fifth Avenue I could see why. The entire street was closed for a parade."

"That was inconvenient," said Horace, frowning slightly.

"Well, you know me," said Mr. Potterton. "I welcome life's little surprises, so I reached into the glove compartment and took out my flag.

"The next thing you know there was a loud crash and a giant brown wave coming toward my car."

"A brown wave?" said Horace doubtfully.

"A *giant* brown wave," said Mr. Potterton. "A molasses truck had been hit, and its contents were pouring out.

"Well," continued Mr. Potterton, "I said to myself, 'Life is too short to get upset over anything as small as a giant wave of molasses covering my car,' so I stayed to enjoy the parade. Until the bees came. Then I thought it prudent to leave."

"That was wise," said Horace, thinking Mr. Potterton's story the most ridiculous of all, and wishing more than ever that he had stayed at home.

The Pottertons fixed what was left of the dinner. It was quite tasty, but Horace had no appetite. He pushed his food around the plate and wondered why the Pottertons had kept him waiting and made up such silly excuses.

"Maybe they just don't like me any more," he thought.

At seven o'clock, the newsboy delivered the evening paper. It missed the front steps, sailed through the open window, and landed in the soup. Horace retrieved it and noticed the headlines.

"Golly!" thought Horace. "Everything they said was true!" Suddenly he felt quite hungry and asked for a second helping.

"It sure is nice eating with Emmaline and her parents," he thought. And Horace was very happy even though there was no chocolate cake.